The Kite That Bridged Two Nations

HOMAN WALSH and the FIRST NIAGARA SUSPENSION BRIDGE

ALEXIS O'NEILL

ILLUSTRATED by
TERRY WIDENER

CALKINS CREEK
AN IMPRINT OF HIGHLIGHTS
Honesdale, Pennsylvania

Whenever wind lifted off the river
and sent the trees to dancing,
I'd itch to fly a kite.

I'd race to the great Niagara,
plumes of mist rising from plunging waters,
wind licking at my face.
A boy like me knew, just *knew*,
which day would be perfect for flying kites.

But my merchant father never understood
a boy like me.
"Put that kite away," my father always said.
"Apply yourself. Your studies must come first."

Studies? This is what I studied—
reading the wind,
calculating lift,
gauging line length. . . .

One winter day, the wind called to me.
I ran to the open cliff above the falls.
Beside thunder and roar and billowing spray,
beneath the crisp blue canopy of sky,
not once did I think of the bone-chilling cold
as my kite soared.

When the sun rode low, the flutter of a handbill caught my eye.
I pulled my kite and wound the string.

KITE-FLYING CONTEST.
$10 PRIZE TO THE FIRST BOY WHOSE KITE STRING SPANS
FROM AMERICA TO CANADA.
TWO NATIONS, ONE BRIDGE—
A RIVER OF COMMERCE FLOWING BETWEEN.

It was signed *Charles Ellet, Jr.*,
and below this engineer's name was sketched a picture of his plan.

My string could start a bridge? My *string* could start a *bridge!*
From that day on, the contest filled my head.

I built a new kite.

First the spars—
thin, supple wood to bend and cross and bind
to make a perfect frame.

And next some twine,
to wind from point to point to point to point
and fasten it securely.

And now the sail,
cut from calico squirreled away in Mother's sewing basket—
stretched and glued tight as a drumskin, then stitched round.
And then a bellyband
tied to the bow
and a bobtail to keep it stable.
And finally,
more than a thousand feet of string to reach across the gorge.

My kite.
My pride.
I called her Union.

And in my head, I saw her bridge the gap.

On the day when winds blew fair and strong,
I wore my woolens thick to dull the bite of winter.

Against the sky, a confetti of kites already played.
Some boys stood on the American bank.
But a boy like me knew the wind's true course.
Canada was the proper place to catch the southwest breeze.

Down
endless
stairs
I clumped
and ferried cross the roiling river.
Up the other side I climbed, my kite clutched tight in hand.

Through snow, on ice, and two miles north,
I took my place above the grasping Whirlpool Rapids.
Don't look down, I told myself.

I set my gaze aloft and launched my kite.

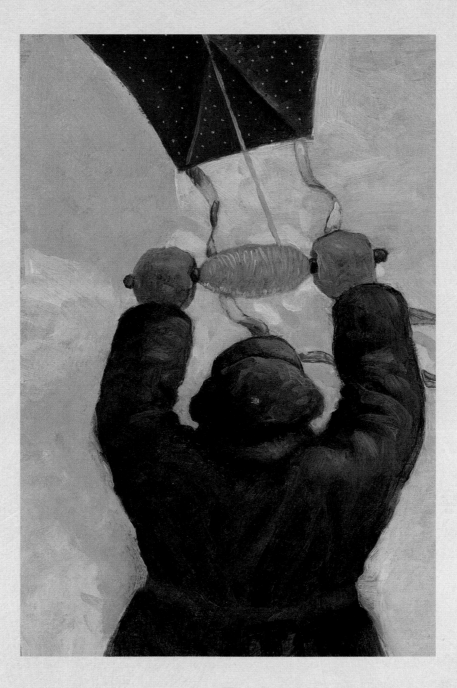

My Union danced, a living thing,
straining, soaring, streaming, free!
My heart danced, too, my spirit lifted,
as if the kite and I were one.

All through the day, my line stayed strong.
People gathered round.
They cheered me on and gave me food
while on my kite my eyes held fast.
My rivals did the same.

As inky night spilled on the sky, the river, and the land,
the cold air claimed our hands, our feet—
and contestants dropped away.
I stomped to keep my body warm
and pulled my woolens tighter.

Then through the dark, two bonfires bloomed—
first one side, then the other.
Crowds were with me! They urged me on.
My purpose blazed anew.

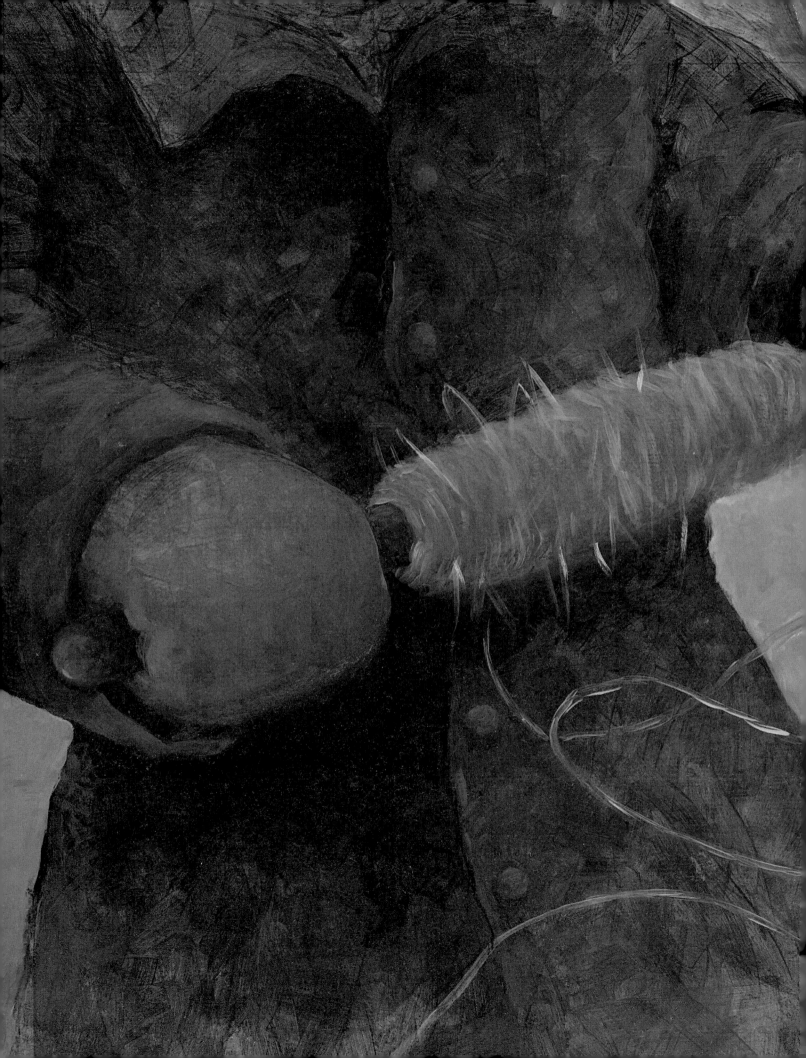

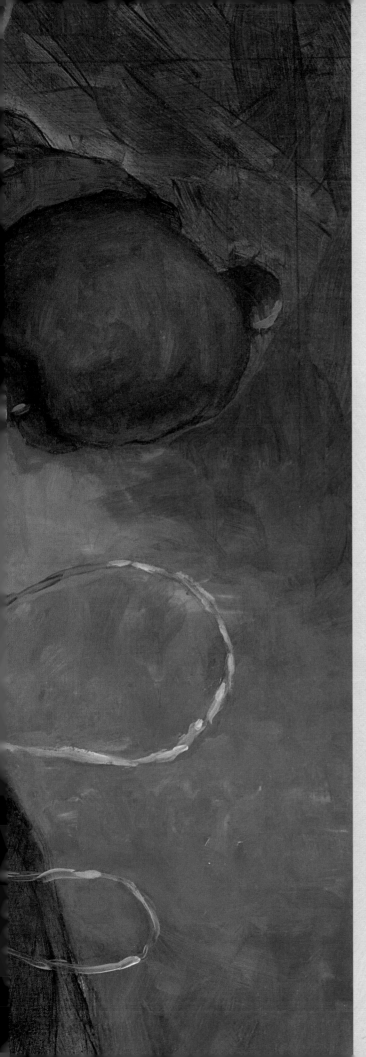

As midnight dropped, so did the wind.
My heart quickened—
a landing near at hand.
Now with a jolt, the string pulled tight.
It caught and held.
America at last!

Then suddenly, a sag, a jerk.
The heavy line went slack!
It snapped on ice below.

No kite.
No cord.
No union.

I could not breathe.
Where had she fallen?
I raced along the icy cliff,
stumbled through the snowy banks,
then to the ferry stairs—
I must rescue my poor Union!
But no ferry ran the river.
With crack and groan,
with creak and moan,
ice choked the river's throat.

For eight long days, ice blocked my journey home.
No ferry to retrieve my kite and start it all again.
Kind folks in Elgin sheltered me,
but all my thoughts were on my kite.
Where was Union?
Had someone rescued her?
Would someone steal her for his own?

Then one day the river cleared,
and with ragged breath,
I hastened home to my family's cries of joy.

My father showed my kite to me.
Her string had snapped,
one spar was bowed,
the tail was gone, the sail was rent.
"But you can work to make it right,"
he said, placing Union in my hands.
He held my gaze and gave a nod,
and to the task I bent with winning in my head.

And when at last a favored wind was blowing,
I grabbed my coat, my hat, my kite,
and to the cliff I ran, then to the ferry, far below.

As we crossed, I looked upstream to falls of
rain and river, rock and tumble,
untamed, unequaled.
I felt its booming, pounding
power in my chest.

When I reached Canadian shores,
I walked to where
cliff faced cliff, the narrowest spot,
and held my Union close.

At the lip, I launched my kite.
Turbulence pitched and pulled
and buffeted her slender frame.
She struggled to gain altitude.
Then at river's center,
wind swept up the gorge,
now smoothed and steady,
and took Union's slender line.
And in that calm, the string spooled out!

As if she knew
her purpose greater than to fly,
Union danced above the rapids.
She danced to heaven's gate,
and then she landed swiftly, safely, strongly
on the American side.

My Union held secure!
The prize was mine.
But better still
was my father in the cheering crowd.

A boy like me had joined two countries!

To the string, my Union's string,
a thicker, stronger line was then attached
and pulled back across—
and then another and another, thicker still,
until at last Charles Ellet, Jr., strung the cable,
and then he built a bridge.
One line—*my line!*—was first to start it all.
A boy like me had started something great.

My kite.
My pride.
My Union.

And though this happened in my youth,
this much is true:
whenever wind lifts off the river
and sends the trees to dancing,
I still itch to fly a kite.

AUTHOR'S NOTE

With mid-nineteenth-century America charging into the Industrial Revolution, Americans believed in harnessing nature to the will of commerce. They worked hard to overcome obstacles for the promise of rich rewards and individual freedoms.

Against this landscape plays the dramatic story of how an ordinary boy named Homan J. Walsh—born in Ireland and raised in Niagara Falls, New York—earned an extraordinary place in history in 1848 by persisting in flying his kite against tremendous odds.

I chose to tell this story from Homan Walsh's point of view because I wanted to express emotions that are not obvious in straight narrative accounts of this event: the wonder of kite-flying, the challenge of proving one's worth to a parent, the exhilaration of being part of history.

WHAT WE KNOW

THE FALLS Niagara Falls straddles the border between the United States and Canada, in New York State and the province of Ontario. On the American side are Bridal Veil and American Falls, and on the Canadian side is Horseshoe Falls. The Niagara River, the source of the falls, is about 35 miles (59 kilometers) long and runs in a south-to-north direction from Lake Erie to Lake Ontario.

THE EVENT On November 9, 1847, The Niagara Falls International Bridge Company (New York) and the Niagara Falls Suspension Bridge Company (Canada) hired engineer Charles Ellet, Jr., to build the first suspension bridge to connect the United States and Canada across the Niagara River, two and a half miles north of Niagara Falls. To generate publicity for this endeavor, Ellet held a kite-flying contest in January 1848, offering a cash prize to the first boy to anchor a string from country to country, 800 feet (244 meters) across the chasm and about 240 feet (73 meters) above the Whirlpool Rapids. The exact dates for the start and completion of this contest are unknown, but it was reported that a half-inch cord was strung on January 31, 1848.

THE WINNER Homan J. Walsh was born in Ireland on March 24, 1831. His family emigrated to America in 1832 and settled in Niagara Falls in 1840. Homan was sixteen years old at the time of the contest. He was said to be the best kite flyer in Niagara Falls.

THE PRIZE Homan Walsh told *Leslie's Weekly* magazine reporter Orrin E. Dunlap in 1897 (forty-nine years after the event) that he won fifty dollars. But bridge supervisor Theodore G. Hulett (later, Judge Hulett), consultant to bridge engineer Charles Ellet, Jr.; and Ellet's nine-year-old daughter, Mary Virginia, who handed the prize to Walsh, reported that the amount was ten dollars. So that is the amount stated in this work.

THE TOWNS Over the years, the names of the towns at either end of the bridge changed. On the U.S. side: from "Bellevue" to "Suspension Bridge" to "Niagara Falls, New York." On the Canadian side: from "Elgin" to "Clifton" to "Niagara Falls, Ontario."

THE WEATHER CHALLENGE The winter of 1848 was particularly harsh. On March 29–30, 1848, two months after the contest, millions of tons of ice became lodged at the source of the Niagara River, completely blocking the channel and causing the falls to go "dry" for thirty hours.

THE FERRY Before the suspension bridge, the only way to cross the Niagara River was by ferryboat. The first ferry, *The Maid of the Mist*, was launched in 1846. After the completion of the bridge, the ferry lost customers but then reestablished itself as a popular tourist-boat operation that continues to this day.

WHAT WE DON'T KNOW

THE CONFLICT There is no record that Homan's father, a merchant and prominent member of the community, disapproved of his son's kite-flying or of his participation in the contest. Dialogue in this book is imagined. However, the census of 1850 shows that Homan lived with another family in Niagara Falls. It's possible that there could have been a conflict within his family or Homan purposely moved away, because he was on the verge of becoming a wage-earning adult.

THE HANDBILL No one has ever found evidence of how the contest was promoted. However, it was common in the 1800s to post handbills, otherwise known as broadsides, for events.

THE KITE Kite historians believe that Homan probably constructed a barn-door kite for the contest. This six-sided kite, covered in a light muslin or calico, was a popular design in the mid-1800s and could withstand strong winds and dampness. Although Homan is reported to have carried "balls of twine," the exact length of the kite's line is unknown.

THE CANADIAN FRIENDS We don't know who sheltered Homan in Canada during the eight days he waited for the ferry to run again.

THE REST OF THE STORY

Engineer Charles Ellet, Jr., staged two dramatic events to show the progress of the Niagara Suspension Bridge.

First, on Monday, March 13, 1848, he pulled himself across the chasm above the whirlpool rapids in an iron basket. The trip took fifteen minutes. Soon after, he charged tourists for the privilege. His daughter, Mary Virginia, was the first female to cross in the basket. On July 29, 1848, after the builders finished a wooden service bridge that was 7.5 feet wide (2.3 meters), Ellet drove a buggy pulled by a high-spirited horse chariot-style across the expanse. One account says Mary Virginia was in the carriage at the time. This opened the temporary suspension bridge, the first across the Niagara Gorge, to carriage and pedestrian traffic. In a bitter dispute over money, Ellet left the project in December 1848 and went on to complete other engineering projects, notably the Wheeling Suspension Bridge over the Ohio River.

In 1852, John Augustus Roebling began replacing Ellet's bridge with the double-decker Niagara Railway Suspension Bridge, using Ellet's bridge as scaffolding. The first passenger train drove across the upper deck on March 8, 1855, marking this as the world's first working railway suspension bridge.

Homan J. Walsh moved to Lincoln, Nebraska, in 1869, where he worked in the real estate business. He died in Nebraska on March 8, 1899. His body was brought back to Niagara Falls, New York, and is buried in Oakwood Cemetery, within the sound of the falls.

NIAGARA SUSPENSION BRIDGE TIMELINE

1847   NOVEMBER 9
Engineer Charles Ellet, Jr., is contracted by The Niagara Falls International Bridge Company (New York) and the Niagara Falls Suspension Bridge Company (Canada) to construct a bridge spanning eight hundred feet across the Niagara River in full view of the falls.

1848   JANUARY 31
Homan Walsh's kite string becomes the first line for the suspension bridge that will join the United States with Canada.

1848   MARCH 13
Ellet is the first to cross the river in an iron basket held by a wire cable.

1848   JULY 29
Ellet erects a service bridge for transporting men and materials across the gorge.

1848   DECEMBER 27
In a dispute over payment, Ellet quits the bridge project.

1851
Engineer John Augustus Roebling is hired to build the Railway Suspension Bridge, a new two-tiered design that holds a railway on one level, pedestrians and carriages on the other level.

1852
Using Ellet's bridge as scaffolding, Roebling completes the lower deck of the new bridge and opens it to pedestrian and carriage travel.

1855   MARCH 8
The first passenger train drives across the upper deck, marking this as the world's first working railway suspension bridge.

1897   AUGUST 27
The Railway Suspension Bridge is replaced by the Steel Arch Bridge, later renamed the Whirlpool Rapids Bridge.

SELECTED SOURCES

PRIMARY SOURCES (PERIODICALS AND DOCUMENTS)
Buffalo Commercial Advertiser and Journal: January 31, 1848; July 31, 1848.
Buffalo Daily Courier: January 31, 1848; February 3, 1848; July 29, 1848.
Buffalo Daily Republic: August 25, 1848.
Buffalo Morning Express: February 10, 1848.
Niagara Chronicle: February 4, 1848.
United States Federal Census: 1850, 1860.
United States Passport Application: Homan J. Walsh, June 17, 1889.

BOOKS
The American Boy's Book of Sports and Games: A Repository of In-and-Out-Door Amusements for Boys and Youth. New York: Dick and Fitzgerald, 1864.

Berton, Pierre. *Niagara: A History of the Falls*. Albany: Excelsior Editions/State University of New York Press, 2009.

Dunlap, Orrin E. "Niagara Falls' Bridges: The Boy Whose Kite First Crossed the Chasm." In *Niagara: Its History, Incidents and Poetry* by Richard L. Johnson. Washington, DC: Walter Neal, 1898.

Irwin, William R. *The New Niagara: Tourism, Technology, and the Landscape of Niagara Falls, 1776–1917*. University Park: Pennsylvania State University Press, 1996.

Lewis, Gene D. *Charles Ellet, Jr.: The Engineer as Individualist, 1810–1862*. Urbana: University of Illinois Press, 1968.

McCullough, David. *The Great Bridge: The Epic Story of the Building of the Brooklyn Bridge*. New York: Simon and Schuster, 1972.

Poole, William, ed. *Landmarks of Niagara County, New York*. Syracuse, NY: D. Mason and Company, 1897.

Seibel, George A. *Bridges over the Niagara Gorge: Rainbow Bridge, 50 Years, 1941–1991; A History*. Niagara Falls, ON: Niagara Falls Bridge Commission, 1991.

Zavitz, Sherman. *It Happened at Niagara: Stories from Niagara's Fascinating Past*. Rev. ed. Niagara Falls, ON: Lundy's Lane Historical Society, 2008.

WEBSITES*

Anes, Jim. "Flying over the Niagara Gorge: The Homan Walsh Challenge at the Niagara International Kite Festival," October 11, 2005. *Niagara Windriders Newsletter*. nwka.blogspot.com/2005/10/flying-over-niagara-gorge-homan-walsh.html.

Bridges over Niagara Falls: A History and Pictorial. niagarafrontier.com/bridges.html#b1.

Robinson, M. "The Kite That Bridged a River," 2005. Homan Walsh Kite Contest. kitehistory.com.

INTERVIEWS

Ames, Peter B. Research specialist, Niagara Falls, New York.

Coley, Jeannette Martyn Cabell. Great-great-granddaughter of Charles Ellet, Jr.

VIDEOS

How to Build a Barn Door Kite. youtube.com/watch?v=wbaF4ESAGCg.*

Remembering Niagara Falls. River's Edge Productions, 2008.

FOR FURTHER EXPLORATION*

Aeolus Curricula. aeoluscurricula.org.

American Kitefliers Association. aka.kite.org.

Niagara Falls State Park.
New York State Office of Parks, Recreation, and Historic Preservation. nysparks.com/parks/46/details.aspx.

Welcome to Ontario's Niagara Parks.
Niagara Parks (Canada). niagaraparks.com.

ACKNOWLEDGMENTS

For supplying expert advice, research material, and support, many thanks to the following people and institutions: REVIEWERS: Meg Albers, director, Aeolus Curricula, Buffalo, New York; Peter B. Ames, research specialist, Niagara Falls, New York; Tom D. Crouch, senior curator, Aeronautics Division, Smithsonian Institution National Air and Space Museum, Washington, D.C.; Barry J. Virgilio, environmental educator, interpretive programs, Niagara Region of the New York State Parks, Niagara Falls, New York; Tom Yots, director, Preservation Buffalo Niagara, Buffalo, New York; Sherman Zavitz, official historian, Niagara Falls, Ontario, Canada. INSTITUTIONS: Buffalo & Erie County Public Library System, New York; Niagara County Genealogical Society, Lockport, New York; Niagara County Historical Society, Lockport, New York; Niagara Falls Public Library, New York; Niagara Falls Public Library, Ontario, Canada; Strong National Museum of Play, Rochester, New York; Ventura County Library, Ventura, California. SPECIAL THANKS TO: Debra Backman's fifth-grade class, 2010–2011, Flory Academy of Sciences and Technology, Moorpark, California; Dorothy Bickford; David Boeshaar; Jeannette Martyn Cabell Coley; Barbara Grzeslo; Joan Hyman; Holly Kunkle; Sherrill Kushner; Susan Measures; Martha Vestecka Miller; Ann Whitford Paul; Dale Redfield; Amy Roebuck; and Carolyn P. Yoder.

In memory of Dorothy Bryden Carpenter—master teacher, friend, and history lover, who knew the roads of New York State like the back of her hand.   —AO'N

For Michael. Believe in yourself and your dreams. Always.   —TW

For information about permission to reproduce selections from this book, please contact permissions@highlights.com.

Calkins Creek, an Imprint of Highlights
815 Church Street, Honesdale, Pennsylvania 18431
Printed in Malaysia

ISBN: 978-1-59078-938-4

Library of Congress Control Number: 2012955629

First edition
10 9 8 7 6 5 4 3 2 1

Designed by Barbara Grzeslo
Production by Margaret Mosomillo
Hand-lettering by David Coulson
The text is set in Palatino.
The illustrations are done in acrylic on chipboard.

* Websites active at time of publication